OLIVER'S ESCAPE

OLIVER'S ESCAPE

by Consuelo Joerns

Four Winds Press   New York

LIBRARY OF CONGRESS CATALOGING IN PUBLICATION DATA

Joerns, Consuelo.
  Oliver's escape.

  Summary: A dog no one wants seizes an opportunity
to escape from a pet store.
  [1. Dogs—Fiction] I. Title.
PZ7.J5901   [E]   81-1904
ISBN 0-590-07817-8   AACR2
Published by Four Winds Press
A division of Scholastic Inc., New York, N.Y.
Copyright © 1981 by Consuelo Joerns
All rights reserved
Printed in the United States of America
Library of Congress Catalog Card Number: 81-1904
1 2 3 4 5 85 84 83 82 81

For
Doctor Bones,
Master Slow
and, of course,
Harold

Nobody wanted Oliver even though day after day
he lay under a big *for sale* sign in a cage in a pet store.

The pet store owner said, "Some dog! He looks like something the cat dragged in. I'll never be able to sell him!" and he slammed the cage shut.

As the days went by all the other dogs in the store
were sold and went off to new homes. But not Oliver.
He just wasn't the kind of dog anyone wanted to own.

One day, after the pet store owner had locked up and gone home, Oliver found his cage left open by mistake and he jumped out of it.

"Help, help! He's getting out! Call the police! The police!
The police!" shouted a parrot. Oliver ran straight across
the pet store to a window. It was open just wide enough for
him to squeeze through onto the street below.

He ran as fast as he could from all the flashing lights
and honking horns until he came to a quiet street with
big, shady trees and brick houses.

He saw children on the street walking their dogs and then
taking them inside. Through the windows he saw the dogs
being fed. "This is where I should live," thought Oliver.
He went up to one door after another and barked, but no one
let him in.

When night came he was still waiting outside. One by one the lights in the houses went out. Everyone had eaten supper and gone to bed.

At last he found a sort of hole under some steps and
crawled into it. Oliver could not read the sign, so he did
not know he was in Tiger's house. He curled up into a ball
and went to sleep.

Oliver awoke with a start to feel two heavy paws pinning him down. The paws had claws. "I'm Tiger," growled a big tomcat. "I can't find my leftover. Did you eat it?" And he dug his claws into Oliver.

"Please don't eat me!" cried the leftover, suddenly
appearing. Oliver wagged his tail because the leftover
looked just like the mouse he had seen in a cage at
the pet store. "I don't blame you for not wanting to eat it,"
said Tiger. "It's full of little bones and not much else."

"*But,*" said Tiger, rolling over, "if you live on the street
like a stray dog and don't eat mice, you'll have to steal
soup bones from the butcher, and then the other stray dogs
will get you. Too bad!" Tiger yawned and went to sleep.

It was daybreak. "Come on," squeaked the mouse, tugging at
Oliver, "I'll show you the way to the butcher shop." When
the mouse got Oliver outside, he told him his name was Moby.

Moby showed Oliver how to sneak in the back door of the
butcher shop. He stood watch and gave a loud SQUEAK
when he saw the butcher coming. Oliver grabbed a huge
bone and bolted out the door.

He fled down the street. But after a while he remembered
Moby so he stopped and wondered if he should go back and
find him. Just then three wild-looking stray dogs came by
and saw the bone. With growly barks they rushed at Oliver.

They chased Oliver up one street and down another and
around the block and through an alley and across a lawn
and down another street. Oliver was worn out. He saw the

door of a house open and someone reach out to pick up a
newspaper. He ran up the steps and through the door just
before it closed!

"Why, you scrungy little dog," said the butler, "how dare
you come in here! Out with you, you and your dirty bone,"
and he picked up Oliver by the scruff of the neck to throw
him out.

But when the butler opened the door, the stray dogs jumped
at it to get inside and at Oliver's bone, so he slammed the
door shut again. "What is that *awful* noise?" called the

mistress of the house. Before the butler could answer, she came to see for herself. But because she had the wrong glasses, she couldn't see very well. "Why, he's just a baby!" she said. "Put him to bed in the nursery—you'll

find a nightgown in the cupboard. First, give him a bath and ask Cook to send up some baby food. It will be nice to have a child in the house again." Oliver shook with fright. His bone was taken away and he was plunged into a tub of hot water and scrubbed with smelly soap.

He was forced to eat gray slop. Then he was put in a
nightgown and tucked so tightly in a crib that he couldn't
move. After that he was left all alone in the dark.

Presently he saw something stir at the foot of the crib.

"Oliver, come on!" whispered a squeaky voice. It was Moby!

"I got in the cellar and climbed up through the walls."

Moby tugged at Oliver's blanket until he struggled out of the crib.

But Oliver was much too big to escape through a mousehole!
They tried the nursery door—it was locked, and the
window was shut. So Oliver chewed up his nightgown and
Moby tried on some clothes he found in an old dollhouse.
Then Moby snuggled under one of Oliver's warm, furry ears
and they both fell asleep.

The next day the butler took Oliver to the park in a baby carriage. "Madam's new charge," he explained to an astonished passerby. Oliver was frightened to see the very

same dogs who had chased him before. They romped around the
baby carriage looking for his bone. They were so rough, they
knocked the butler down. Then they bumped into the carriage
and set it racing down the hill, faster and faster.

It went right over the bank of a small, winding river and
with a loud SPLASH! fell in. "Good riddance!" said the
butler, who picked himself up and went home.

Oliver floated out of the carriage all tangled up in baby clothes and thrashed about the river yelping. Twice his head went under before he felt something grab him and pull him into a small boat.

"Why, you're not a baby at all. You're a dog!" said the boy who had saved him. Oliver licked the boy's face. Then he ran up and down the boat barking. Where was Moby? Where was Moby? All he could see was the half-drowned carriage floating downstream, almost out of sight.

He jumped right back into the river again, and paddling
with his paws, he swam as fast as he could after the sinking
carriage. Moby was so glad to see him, he made a flying leap
and landed on Oliver's head. Oliver swam back to the boy.

"Bravo!" cried the boy, pulling them aboard. "You saved
your friend!" He lifted up the tiny mouse and said, "I
think I'll call you Moby because you came out of the waves
like the great whale, Moby Dick." Moby gave a little bow.
"And I'll call you Oliver because that's my most favorite
name." Oliver wagged his tail.

Oliver thought he heard the boy say, "I wish you were
my dog and *my* mouse," so he jumped all over the boy, licking
his face. "Are you sure you don't belong to anyone?" said
the boy quite clearly. Oliver almost danced — he hopped
about on his hind legs, barking excitedly. Suddenly he tripped

and fell overboard! This so rocked the boat that the boy
lost his balance and fell in too. But he didn't care. He
and Oliver splashed around in the water, laughing and
yelping. "Look at Moby," said the boy, "he's still in the
boat! Let's get in too, and all go home and EAT!"

And so they all went down the winding river in the little
boat to the boy's house and had a feast such as only true
and extremely hungry friends can have.

THE END